I0612873

Walking

with

Divine Intervention

Inspirational Poetry
for the Heart Mind and Soul

B. Chuck Thomas
"TheOldPoetHimself"

3G Publishing, Inc.
Loganville, Ga 30052
www.3gpublishinginc.com
Phone: 1-888-442-9637

First published by 3G Publishing, Inc. November, 2015

ISBN: 9781941247211

Printed in the United States of America

Acknowledgements

Thank you to my family and friends for the continued support and inspirational words. Thank you to all of those who have opened their hearts and minds to the poetry. Thank you to my wife and daughter for the consistent walk with me and the Lord.

Thank you most of all Jesus Christ for the words and phrases.

Introduction

The poems following were inspired through actual experiences, meditation and personal reflection. Some of the poems are filled with emotion that resulted from personal friends' and relatives' trials and struggles. Some poems offer a different insight on praise and worship. Some of the poetry strikes to the soul of the Christian as we attempt to fully live the Word. The divine intervention is evident with the strong spiritual references. As you read the poetry, I am confident that you will be internally blessed and forever changed. Enjoy!

The Call

We need to heed the Word! On our walk, we must be guided by the Light of Jesus Christ!

B. Chuck Thomas

"TheOldPoetHimself"

Table of Contents

All Power

In the Palm of Your Hand
Within the Strength of Your Will
Resting in the Knowledge of Your Mercy
Being relaxed in Your Grace that I feel

I know You have formed my whole future
I know Your Will has been cast
I know You continue to love me
I know You have forgiven my past

I know Your Truth is unending
I know Your Word, time won't outlast
I know You get me over temptation
I know I must pray when I fast

Yes love on me My Dear Savior
Shield my life, cover me with the Blood
Give to me Your Holy Understanding
In my soul let the Wisdom please flood

As I come to You on my knees
Give me courage to do what I say
My words pledge to be in Your Kingdom
Now Lord help me walk day to day

Psalm 91:1

He that dwelleth in the secret place of the most High shall abide under the shadow of the Almighty.

Appointed Shepherd

Tell me something please Pastor
Tell me how to see God's Face
Tell me how to hear direction
Tell me how to seek His Grace

Sir, I know there're things in scripture
And I know some verse and book
But I still need clearer meaning
Can you tell me where to look

Pastor, can you solve my problem
I do want to know God's Plan
Pastor you are my earthly leader
You can help me....yes you can

My dear brother I have heard you
I know your heart and what you seek
Your desire is worthy I will help you
Stay pure of heart and remain meek

My dear brother our Holy Father
Knows our mind and spirit too
And He gave a message to me
The Holy Spirit dwells in you

Keep on praying for understanding
You'll gain wisdom and discernment too
Stay in His Will and all The Meaning
Will reveal "Itself" to you

Zachariah 11:17

Woe to the idol shepherd that leaves the flock! The sword shall be upon his arm, and upon his right eye: his arm shall be clean dried up, and his right eye shall be utterly darkened.

Blind Mind

I am a good person
I go to church when I can
That alone shows that I am right
I'm not like the sinful man

I have not killed anybody
I know that is a sin
So I'm really living fine
In this life I will win

I say a few wrong words
From time to time when I'm mad
But I still do good for others
I even cheer up people if they're sad

You see I'm just like an angel
Nobody is perfect in this land
I thank the spirits up above
And when I'm troubled He's my man

I don't need the church
I have a good job and health
I send them an offering sometimes too
I do thank God for my wealth

I am not as bad as my neighbor
He says mean things to his wife
Maybe that's why I'm living good
I don't worry with such strife

I do love to party down
What's really wrong with my song
You have to enjoy life to the fullest
I'm not worried with what is wrong

I expect to see heaven
Why not, I do better than some
I've been told that I'm righteous
Invite me to prayer...sometimes I'll come

I see things the right way
I see things how they seem to be
I'm just as good as the next
Don't sit and pass judgement on me!!

2 Corinthians 4:3, 4

But if our gospel be hid, it is hid to them that are lost: In
whom the God of this world hath blinded the minds of them
which believe not, lest the light of the glorious gospel of
Christ, who is the image of God should shine upon them.

Careful Praying

Oh man is such an oddly creature
Praying for faith then what's to come
Yet in an unfaithful tone yet present
The test to pass for faith is from

The man is such an oddly creature
Praying for wisdom then what's to come
Yet in an information to gather Jesus
The test to pass for wisdom's done

To gain more measure of faith that's given
To gain the power that faith does hold
Will take a challenge to that faith
And then the test of faith behold

To gain a bit of King Solomon's wisdom
To gain the deeper wisdom of mind
Will take a circumstance of choices
And then the test result to find

So man as we pray and we'll continue
Consider what we need for bliss
And as we go to God for Holy things
Then know the tests we cannot miss

1 Corinthians 2:4, 5

And my speech and my preaching was not with enticing words of man's wisdom, but in demonstration of the Spirit and of power: That your faith should not stand   in the wisdom of men, but in the power of God.

Clearer Me

Up from out of a shadow
Of so much pain and much self-doubt
Thinking clearer and with a purpose
Realizing what this walk is all about

Challenging myself to learn the more
And get clearer understanding of Your Word
Knowing I can build on a foundation
Of Your Scriptures I already heard

Gaining some wisdom, gaining some hope
Again seeing things so much clearer
Dealing with this world day by day
Working so that You Lord I am nearer

My life is changing I'm standing firm
My feet are planted on Your Ground
My purpose clearer my thinking clearer
My life in Your Will is now found

Create In Me

Help me now Lord with Your Strength
Help me Lord on this walk start
Give me what I need to go forth
My goal is to be pure of heart

Give me Lord the wisdom I need
Give me Lord the knowledge too
Help me Jesus I love you deeply
My goal dear Lord is to see You

Help me to increase in You Lord
Help me make change from me to You
Give me the Holy Spirit now Lord
I ask forgiveness, I'll repent too

My goals are in reach I have Your Tools Lord
Now seeing You and pure of heart
Keep giving me Your Loving Spirit Lord
And in this **walk** I won't depart

Matthew 5:8

Blessed are the pure in heart: for they will see God.

Don't Move

Get me ready to receive
The wonders of Your Infinite Love
And the fullness of a blessing
That gently comes from Up Above

Clean my heart and wipe my spirit
Make me free of sin You see
Pour out of grace Your gentle mercies
Let them flow down over me

In the calmness, no the stillness
No, the peace I do desire
Please my mind Lord and my spirit
As You quench the tempting fire

The Word of Truth You place so deeply
Shields my soul from thoughts of past
As I plant myself in oneness
Into the Kingdom now at last

Yes, My Father I am ready
I am open to Your Will
Give me now the Holy Guidance
I **receive** You now....*I'll be still*

2 Chronicles 20:17

You will not have to fight this battle. Take up your positions; stand firm and see the deliverance the LORD will give you, Judah and Jerusalem. Do not be afraid; do not be discouraged. Go out to face them tomorrow, and the LORD will be with you.

Eye Opener

Does it have to take a struggle
To finally want to seek Your Face
Does it always take being broken
To pray for mercy and some grace

In my living and growing daily
In my trying to make it day to day
In my falling short in some things
In my wondering where is my way

You have taken me from me
You God have taken from my thought
You have pulled out from my thinking
You God have left room to be taught

I did praise You in my abundance
I did praise You in my heart
But maybe selfish pride did stall me
From work in the Kingdom then to start

With this stripping of some worldly things
Then a reviewing of my way
With an evaluation of my inner self
Left no words for me to say

So, I thank You Holy Father
For the spiritual adjustment during my strife
And I realize through these changes
Lord, You have saved my eternal life

Matthew 20:32, 33

And Jesus stood still, and called them, and said, What will ye
that I shall do unto you? They say unto him, Lord, that our
eyes may be opened.

God's Petal

A time of gentle inner peace
The smell of jasmine...rose
A touch with such a calming feel
Doubtful thoughts are stopped and froze

Lord I'm open and I need You so
Lord help me on this walk
Lord I'm standing at this trial in life
Lord change my thought, my talk

The Word of God to please the heart
The scripture to feed the mind
A verse of words to soothe the soul
God's there with you through time

The pressures of this daily life
Weighs on the nerves so true
Implant Your calming Spirit Lord
Implant Your Holy Wisdom too

The discernment of Your Knowledge Lord
Awareness of Wisdom builds
All the faith I'll need to pass this time
And Your Will to then Fulfill

Psalm 85:10

Love and faithfulness meet together;
righteousness and peace kiss each other.

High View

Your man has done things with that mind Lord
Allowing him to move upon the air
And using worldly knowledge that flows through Lord
Ignoring all Your Miracles without a care

Yet as my eyes see all Your Splendid Wonder
I do see all Your handy work indeed
And as I glare around I feel Your Glory
And Lord I feel the presence that I need

Oh come to me my Savior rest my spirit
Oh love on me Your Wonders I behold
Oh Father bless me as I raise my knowledge
Oh Jesus You're the One that soothes the soul

The open sky and the mountains down below me
The roaring of the ocean and the sea
The living with the blessings from You Father
And know that You alone...created me

To rest within the peaceful morning glory
To You my God for this I give You praise
And as I smile on all Your World around me
I'm pleased You smiled on me to go my way

Thank You Jesus

Hungry

The Kingdom of God
Could be described as a good food
Something that we love to indulge
And then so alter the mood

A heavenly feeling
Something far sweeter than cake
A place that like a dessert celebrates us
And like icing a taste we should take

The Kingdom can be like the best part
Of the pie......the crust
And to dwell in the Kingdom
Into the Word's knowledge is a must

We must strive for the Kingdom
For reality now.....not a dream
For the Lord cools our temptations
And soothes the soul like ice cream

So as we strive to be better
And for the Kingdom we feel
We must obtain the Lord's blessing
And treat the Kingdom as a meal..........***Eat Up***

Luke 1:53

He has filled the hungry with good things
but has sent the rich away empty.

Intention Good

Awakening the spirit from inside....

New Beginnings with the purpose to abide
Living my life totally with You Lord
Your Truth I will not hide

Being so close to Your Love Lord
In You I will continue to confide
Controlling my flesh to walk with
The Holy Spirit side by side
Holding on tight to Your Word Lord
And on Your Grace I will ride

Staying strong in Your Knowledge
So to sin I will not slide
My plan is to stay planted in Your Power
So over this rough time I will glide

I know I'm changed Lord...I'm smiling
Because last night I just cried
My faith is on You My Lord
Not on the devil...because he lied

I want You fully Lord
I will continue to abide
I Thank You because I know for me
Your Precious Son, He died

Romans 8:2

For the law of the Spirit of life in Christ Jesus hath made me free from the law of sin and death.

It's Later Than You Think

How can you play with the devil
And then hope he will always behave
And then you find yourself praying
So that your soul might be saved

How did you not know the vision
It was in your eyes, can't you see
And yes you were wrong to be in it
Instead you think it's them and not me

"I can always handle myself"
"I can deal with whatever comes down"

You are only strong in your own sight
Look again 'cause you're flat on the ground

And as you realize your nature
Oh yes you are simple.....in sin
Change the way you worship on Jesus
Change the way you let the Spirit in

Now take the biggest first step
Be honest, you know you are living so wrong
Come now and get right with Jesus
Time is short...you don't have that long

Ephesians 4:25-27

Therefore each of you must put off falsehood and speak truthfully to your neighbor, for we are all members of one body. "In your anger do not sin": Do not let the sun go down while you are still angry, and do not give the devil a foothold.

Jesus Would

What would Jesus do the question asks
How would Jesus deal with loss?
Would Jesus clap aloud or just shake His Head
As people wear their "special cross"

What would Jesus do from here with us?
Would Jesus Christ just be at ease?
How would Jesus frown or look in shock
To see present day Pharisees

What would Jesus do what would He Say?
To see all the <u>Christian</u> sin
What would Jesus do how would He feel
To see temptation win again!

What would Jesus do what would He Say?
How would Jesus react just so
As we ask this Jesus...we must get prepared
The response we'll need to know....

What would Jesus do the question asks
I don't think He would keep the same
For if Jesus Christ would **do the do**
He'd expect better from those of His Name

2 Thessalonians 1:12

That the name of our Lord Jesus Christ may be glorified in you, and ye in him, according to the grace of our God and the Lord Jesus Christ.

Jezebel Spirit

Lord help me walk to You
Help me flee this spirit real
This spirit is coming against You
This spirit confuses how I feel

Lord help me to remove this spirit
This spirit comes all against *Your* men
It comes unto us like a victim
But then this spirit causes us to sin

This spirit comes in a lovely form
You would think its purpose is from Above
This spirit says that "The Word" it follows
But then corrupts the church that You love

Oh Lord You have dealt with this before
Of course You win and that is true
This spirit Lord keeps changing forms
You know its power is not of You

Lord give us the strength to overcome
This spirit loves to manipulate
This spirit needs attention that it yearns
And causes the discord that You hate

I'll stand and keep Your Holy Word
I'll take the lead and will not fail
Help us defeat this evil spirit
It is the spirit of Jezebel

Revelation 2:20

Notwithstanding I have a few things against thee, because thou suffers that woman Jezebel, which called herself a prophetess, to teach and to seduce my servants to commit fornication, and to eat things sacrificed unto idols.

Just not Understanding

I pray all the time to You My Lord
I work to stay inside Your Will
I lift my face to always thank You
I know for my sin Jesus was killed

I know to keep on reading Lord
I know how not to sin
I walk with You and resist temptation
I don't let the evil stuff creep in

I make sure that I'm present Lord
I dwell inside Your House
I do all that I'm asked My God
I honor commitment and my spouse

I do give You my time Dear Lord
I give offerings of my best
I just get off the knowledge path
I may not have wisdom for the test

I still hurt even though I'm sure
I know through faith You heal
I still am left a bit confused, yet
I know my eternal life is sealed

Lord even though I know great things
I still have so much doubt
Am I just being too shallow Lord
Not realizing what Your Truth is all about

What can I do to help my mind
Can I get clearer on today
Help me get stronger my Dear Lord
Please help me find my way

Psalm 119:33, 34

Teach me, LORD, the way of your decrees,
that I may follow it to the end.
Give me understanding, so that I may keep your law
and obey it with all my heart.

Keep Me

I need You to help me now Lord
I don't know what else to do
I need You to rescue myself
Lord I'm depending all on You

It's not a sinful situation
That I now find myself in
This time of unknowing is just so strong
I need You to be a Special Friend

Guide my next move please Lord
Be a filter for all things I see
Give me some wisdom to overcome
Help me get where I need to be

Oh Lord please keep me on the path
Into Your Kingdom this I can
Instill Your Truth and Holy Power
Help me to be a better man

Oh Father this world has me shaky
Even though I know "all" You do control
Just keep my mind and heart clear Lord
And yes, keep watch over my soul

Proverbs 2:6

For the LORD giveth wisdom: out of his mouth cometh
knowledge and understanding.

Love Alone

To grasp the fleeting concept
Of other people not just me
Others existing in the world around
People in places I can't see

It will never come to a selfish mind
That others are here too
And I go on worrying about myself
Do I even care about you

Lord, what is this sinful nature in
What is this...is it pride
Or Lord not pride but an evil heart
That lies right there inside

Lord what if any can be done
You said all's lost no love
So getting everything out of this life
Can't get your soul Above

Lord, You said no matter what we do
It's nothing if there's no love
Not the love that keeps a body close
But the Love that's from Above

Place in the mind, place in the heart
Your Love place in the soul
Give us the love to love our fellow man
And You Lord something...to then behold

1 John 3:10

This is how we know who the children of God are and who the children of the devil are: Anyone who does not do what is right is not God's child, nor is anyone who does not love their brother and sister.

Mirror of Me

The temptor is on my heel Lord
The deceiver wants my joy
The liar is trying to keep me
That spirit wants my mind to be his toy

The truth that I am seeing Lord
Is a lie and not from You
It cannot be the absolute truth Lord
If it changes the way that I trust in You

So I am looking deeper on this Lord
So I know my mind is too weak
So I know I have to focus more
So I know that it is You I must seek

I realize I need to grow quickly Lord
My level of understanding cannot remain in doubt
My body is present but my mind is still searching Lord
I'm finally in full grasp of what Your Word is about

I will now have control of my spirit Lord
To be in line with my body and heart
I will stay on the path of this Truth Lord
And from You Lord I will not depart

1 Peter 5:8

Be alert and of sober mind. Your enemy the devil prowls around like a roaring lion looking for someone to devour.

More Being

On wings of eagles I will soar
With strength and power of a lion's roar
Into Your Kingdom Lord for You I do adore
What need I do more
To You I implore

Pray more Study more Praise more
Hear more Read more Witness more
Love more Feel more Teach more
Do more See more Smile more
Write more Share more Visit more
Sing more Wait more Work more
Watch more Listen more Think more
Trust more Obey more Know more

Be more than before
Being more can open the door
To the Kingdom of God.....forever more

For it is You my Lord
I do adore
I will strive to love You........more

1 Chronicles 29:11

Yours, LORD, is the greatness and the power
and the glory and the majesty and the splendor,
for everything in heaven and earth is yours.
Yours, LORD, is the kingdom;
you are exalted as head over all.

New Seed

A NEW LIFE IN THE WORLD
ANOTHER SPIRIT TO LEARN AND GROW
ANOTHER SAINT TO BUILD THE KINGDOM
ANOTHER LOVING HEART FOR YOU TO KNOW

A NEW BREATH THAT HITS THE AIR
NEEDS THE THINGS THAT YOU PROVIDE
A NEW LIFE THAT NEEDS YOUR GUIDANCE
AND WITH YOUR WORD LIVE SIDE BY SIDE

A SMALL BABY JUST A CHILD
A SMALL MIRACLE AND SPECIAL JOY
THE HOPE OF LIFE THE WISH FOR LOVE
AND ALL YOUR WILL TO THEN EMPLOY

AS THE NEWNESS IS HOPE FOR TOMORROW
A FRESH BEGINNING AND GREAT REVEAL
PUT IN THE POSITION OF SERVING YOU
AND IN YOUR WILL THEN BE FULFILLED

1 John 3:9

No one who is born of God will continue to sin, because God's seed remains in them; they cannot go on sinning, because they have been born of God.

New Walking

Walk in Strength **Walk** in Power
Walking in Knowledge
Hour by the hour

Walk in Love **Walk** in Peace
Walking in Forgiveness
The past things release

Walk in Wisdom **Walk** without pain
Walking in the Scriptures
Avoiding the rain

Walk in Truth **Walk** in Light
Walking in the Word
Do what is Right

Walk in Discernment **Walk** in Salvation
Walking in Courage
Healing the nation

Walk in Body **Walk** in Mind
Walking with the Lord
Leave the devil behind

Proverbs 28:26

Those who trust in themselves are fools,
but those who walk in wisdom are kept safe.

No Much Cry

Lord as I go from day to day
Not knowing what is next I have to fear
Lord feeling so anxious for a blessing
I still can't pause to shed a tear

The act of crying soothes the nerves
And yes some tears can ease the pain
Lord I'm lost looking for Your Will
I'm wet but can't get out of the rain

All I want to do is move
By moving I'm hoping to a better place
Not a physical move Lord...You know
But a spiritual change to save my face

Lord I don't have a need to quit
Lord I have lasted more than some
Lord I have questioned myself so much
Lord I have made my senses numb

Lord please allow my eye to tear
Lord please let my heart release some swell
Lord please renew me a better self
Lord please...I have only **You** to tell

Thank You Lord I pray to Thee
My sorrow in mind for no one to hear
And Lord just bless me in this moment
My Savior...let me just shed a tear

Psalm 126:5

They that sow in tears shall reap in joy.

No Shaky Walk

I am standing on the promise of
A better life You said would come
I am hoping with the spirit
That I've fled the sin I'm from

I feel I'm at a point now Lord
When something needs to break
I'm being patient and I'm trusting You
But Lord this worry I can't fake

Is now a time for coming through
Is now a time for change
Is now a time to overcome
Is now my blessing within range

Be with me Lord take hold my hand
Remove the cloud of doubt
Bring me strength and share Your Power
Prove what this faith's about

I'm walking now, I keep the steps
Lord order true my way
I'm not just standing...I'm standing strong
Please Lord keep clear my way

Within Your Love and Mercy Lord
Within Your Hand of grace
Guide me Lord and love me true
I'll strive to seek Your Face

Zachariah 3:6,7

And the angel of the LORD protested unto Joshua, saying, Thus said the LORD of hosts; If thou wilt walk in my ways, and if thou wilt keep my charge, then thou shalt also judge my house, and shalt also keep my courts, and I will give thee places to walk among these that stand by.

Only One

The culture of the western world
The regard of Who's supreme
The being that the worship heralds
The truth to hold it seems

The Subject does bring roll of eyes
The Subject still suggests
The Subject and the focus of
The Subject should only get the best

It's Jesus not the other god
The Subject, the Supreme Being
The Worship heralds the Holy One
The Truth all eyes are seeing

No other thing no other stuff
No other spirit...no one but He
The All in all the worship to
The One God that's all to be

Do worship and give up the praise
Do worship from the knees
Do honor the only Spirit True
Do only call on Jesus......Please

Philippians 2:10,11

That at the name of Jesus every knee should bow, of things in heaven, and things in earth, and things under the earth; And that every tongue should confess that Jesus Christ is Lord, to the glory of God the Father.

Open and Shut

Open your mind to what is real
And allow your eye to see the sight
Hear what you want but let the ear decide
The sound of what is right

Open your heart to what is real
And allow your pulse to beat so true
Move forward with steps to move your way
Allow His Will to lead you too

Open your mouth to what is real
And allow your words to praise His Name
Move your arms about and spread your hands
To receive all the gifts and claim

Open your soul to what is real
And allow the Spirit to dwell within
As you release yourself to *God's whole love*
Then close all up around **Your Friend**

Proverbs 18:24

One who has unreliable friends soon comes to ruin
but there is a friend who sticks closer than a brother.

Open World

Jesus I stand before You ready
And in Your presence I fear Your Face
I know right now I need to change
Realize my sins and find my place

I'll find the place for me Oh Savior
In Your Kingdom and by Your Word
I'm working now to turn back sin
I'm ready now for Your Voice is heard

The world is sinful and so sinful
The world is seemingly void of You
The world is all about the world
The world has eyes yet see not true

The world is sinful yes so sinful
The world is sinning against You
The world is all about the world
The world has ears yet hear not true

Jesus I am Yours please heal me
I'm not of this world...***I'm of You***
My heart and mind are transformed fully
I hear and see Your Will so true

Hebrews 9:26

For then must he often have suffered since the foundation of the world: but now once in the end of the world hath he appeared to put away sin by the sacrifice of himself.

Pledging Myself

I keep on working in Your Will
Not taking heart to what I see
I know I have to keep the Faith
While so much sin is around me

My Lord I have to guard my mind
The devil wants for me to hear
All sorts of sounds that are so sinful
Lord, I have to cover up my ears

Jesus I am still going to follow
All the scriptures on my walk
I realize if I'm in The Word
Out from my mouth will be good talk

My Lord I'm opened up to You
I do seek You more each day
With the Holy Spirit dwelling in me
I will not waiver from Your Way

I'll keep on striving on the path
For Your Truth Lord I will stand
I put no other god before You
And let no evil touch my hand

Jesus I do love You Lord
My Christ I come to You and pray
I need You as my Holy Savior
Give me Your Power on Today

Romans 15:13

Now the God of hope fill you with all joy and peace in believing, that ye may abound in hope, through the power of the Holy Ghost.

Poet's Poem

As I write a word to You Oh Lord
And a phrase does come to mind
I allow the pen to just keep moving
And the words each just seem to find

I look on in an amazement
As the phrase becomes a rhyme
And then I pause and wait for guidance
To see what the result will be this time

I think of how You gently help me
And yes a title comes to need
With a pause and quick reflection
Gives the title to which I heed

Lord I wonder where You want the poems
Lord what is Your Plan to see
Then I look on how the words change life
And know it's not the words from me.

So I thank You for the chance Dear Lord
To be used in Your Plan
And yes Dear Lord I know the verses
Have helped me be a better man

2 Timothy 2:21

If a man therefore purge himself from these, he shall be a vessel unto honor, sanctified, and meet for the master's use, and prepared unto every good work.

Praise and Worship

When the hour is early AM
And the sun just starts to rise
Comes a moment when I should be worshipped
When all the tears pour out of eyes

As the day goes later to midnight
As the work of life has stalled
Comes a moment when I should be worshipped
When on all knees men should fall

There are minutes and yes hours
Passing has moved from dawn to night
Came a time when I should have been worshipped
When through your day you tried to live right

It is never too late to praise Me
It is never too early to praise
It is never too often to praise Me
Did I not create you for the purpose of praise

I want to be worshipped always
I want to be the "All" in your praise
I want to be the Spirit inside you
I want you to worship Me for always

Psalm 109:30

With my mouth I will greatly extol the LORD;
in the great throng of worshipers I will praise him.

Quench Please

How does a man walk through the
.....Fire of life
Without the smell of smoke
And then how does that man stand
.....Up to doubt
From all his close in folk

What have You planted, if indeed
To make this man stand strong
With hope and faith from words he's read
That lead can not be wrong

And yet the fire consumes the mind
The fire does singe the soul
And even though the smoke remains
Your Spirit can make him whole

The walk through life the questions asked
Your Ears have heard a few
With all the prayers that come to mind
Your Wisdom still holds true

So what then Lord, must men just wait
Keep praying....holding fast
And look to **You** to clear the air
And ease the burn at last!!

A prayer, a song, a thoughtful hymn
These things do soothe the pain
Oh Lord be clear
Remove the fire
Allow Your Will to appear....so plain

1 Peter 4:12

Dear friends, do not be surprised at the fiery ordeal that has come on you to test you, as though something strange were happening to you.

Re-Living

Lord You never hide Your Holy Truth
You always do reveal
With the reading of Your Holy Word
Such pain the words do heal

Behind the wall of living true
Just pass the door of shame
With acts of sin we dance around
Never calling the sin its name

Lord living can be done with ease
It's the way we live that's rough
With the satisfaction of selfish lust
Causes each breath to be so tough

Your Commandments Lord do come to mind
How to live....that is our guide
With a glancing look but no comprehend
Leaves Your People with sin to hide

You Lord left a means to overcome
You Lord loved and...One was sent
You Lord gave us steps to better lives
You Lord said "ask"...*forgiveness* and **repent!**

Mark 1:4

And so John the Baptist appeared in the wilderness, preaching a baptism of repentance for the forgiveness of sins.

Simple Focus

Focusing my eyes to see Truth
Guiding my body past all sin
Going through this life is a struggle
I'm having to clear my heart from within

I keep on changing my focus
Yet my drive is to keep it simple
All I want to do is live righteous
Yet temptation irritates like a pimple

Lord I know I need only You
Lord I know I need not to sin
Lord I know my future is with You
Lord I know in You life begins

Lord I know where my focus should be
Lord I know it's right on Your Way
Lord I know it's simple to do
Lord I know yet still refocus each day

I will indeed keep it simple
I will focus like I never did before
I will live this life here much better
I will read The Word and pray more

Psalm 25:5

Lead me in thy truth, and teach me: for thou art the God of my salvation; on thee do I wait all the day.

Small Word

How do you call yourself a Christian
But you spew out so much hate
How can you say "be patient with God"
Yet for I minute you can't wait

How can you call yourself a saint
But your thoughts seem straight from hell
How do you attempt to remain holy
But yet daily in this fail

How can a man sew many seeds
And never think he has to reap
How does that man say "I Love Jesus"
But God's Commandments cannot keep

How does a woman raise her voice
To come against the Words of God
How did she get so far from being a jewel
And the Truth be so apart

It is bad and it is deadly
It has a stench that starts within
A selfish heart...some foolish pride
A little word that is called...sin

Proverbs 20:15

There is gold, and a multitude of rubies: but the lips of knowledge are a precious jewel.

Teach Lord

Today I felt an awful hurt
From someone I call a friend
I pondered to why it bothered me so
And when all the hurt would end

I remember what You taught me Lord
On how I should forgive
And I thought of so how it's hard to do
And how indeed I need to live

I remember what you taught me Lord
On how I should forgive
And I thought of so hard it was for me
And how indeed I need to live

I remember what You taught me Lord
On how you forgave me
And I realize how I hurt You so
With the sins from me You see

I remember what You taught me Lord
And I forgave my friend so true
I thought of how "to not forgive is sin"
So I did forgive.....because I love You

Forgive me for I sin against Thee

Luke 17:3,4

Take heed to yourselves: If thy brother trespass against thee, rebuke him; and if he repent, forgive him. And if he trespass against thee seven times in a day, and seven times in a day turn again to thee, saying, I repent; thou shalt forgive him.

The Comforter

Is there ever rest for the weary
Is it only a thought
Why worry in this life of its sin
And we've already been bought

In Sunday School we did show
And seems like the teachers we taught
With a mindset of wonder and amazement
For something good that we sought

If we don't learn a new lesson
From so much sin that was wrought
Can a new freshness be upon us
Would then Christ's death be for naught

Let us rest in God, Get strength in Christ
We'll win the battle that's fought
Help me now Jesus, hold this Truth
The Holy Spirit is caught

Isaiah 49:13

Sing, O heavens; and be joyful, O earth; and break forth into singing, O mountains: for the LORD hath comforted his people, and will have mercy upon his afflicted.

Trying to Please

What does it take to please You God
What does it take to serve
What does it take to make You smile
What does Your Love deserve

What does it take to walk with You
What does it take to pray
What does it take to fulfill Your Will
What does praise do for Your Day

I want to make You proud of me
I want to lift Your Name
I want to be so strong in You
I want to so be not the same

I want to change my sinful tone
I want to change my view
I want to study to be approved
I want so to be close to You

What will it take to see Your Face
I want to know my part
What does it take for eternal life
I know in Your Word...**that is a start!**

Luke 9:23

And he said to them all, If any man will come after me, let him deny himself, and take up his cross daily, and follow me.

Understand Me

The movement to honor Your Name
The energy to praise You
The thoughts of worship and spiritual cleanse
Are the reason You have made us

Yet Lord with this life's worry in
The things to do to live
Consume and drain Your Child to end
It is You to us forgive

With nothing left an empty tank
On knees we bow to love
And with a thought and fighting sleep
To acknowledge You Above

And even if we start at dawn
To give first breath to You
The thoughts and prayer go quickly pushed
By task we're soon to do

Have mercy Lord...You always do
Have grace Lord to my name
I'm working at this praising thing
While trying to keep my sane

I thank You for that mercy too
I thank You for Your Grace
I'm weary from this worldly struggle
I'll keep praying to seek Your Face

Hold me Lord!!

Psalm 106:1

Praise ye the LORD. O give thanks unto the LORD; for he is good: for his mercy endures forever.

Weight Loss

What is this on my shoulder Lord
What is this on my back
What is this giving me doubt today
To not stand straight but be so slack

What is this on my shoulder Lord
What is this on my back
What is this causing me such sorrow
Can I resist this strong attack

The devil is on my shoulder Lord
The demon is on my back
What can I do to move this temptor
Will Your Word keep me on track

This weight on my head and shoulders now
Past sins and shameful thought
Remove this pressure...I know it's the devil Lord
I'm forgiven through Jesus...my soul is bought

I stand in courage with You today
Oh Lord You uplift me
I'm finding strength within Your arms
I will lose this weight You'll see

1 Corinthians 16:13

Watch ye, stand fast in the faith, quit you like men, be strong.

Who Calling

Calling on all Christians
Who live by the Holy Name
All Christians who keep on thriving
In this evil world all the same

Calling on all Christians
Please stay true to all you do

Calling on all Christians
Keep on studying and praying too

Yes, Lord we have to call all Christians
It's getting tough to make the stand
Keep giving strength to us Christians
We will keep working from Your Hand

Calling on all Christians
Keep ready for the temptor's fight
As we call on all the Christians
Stay on the path and do what's right

Calling on all my Christian brothers
Calling on all Christian sisters too
We have to now more than ever
Call on our Savior to see us through

Bless us Jesus

1 Peter 4:16

Yet if any man suffer as a Christian, let him not be ashamed;
but let him glorify God on this behalf.

Willing Plea

Oh God why do I feel so weak
When in Your Strength I walk
And why do I not have words
When from Your Word I talk

Why do You hide Your Will
Can You just reveal Your Plan
Why can't You make it clear
You have all power in Your Hand

Please God show me my fate
I'm struggling and turned around
I know I've been here before
But seems Your Will is still unfound

Yes I can't see Your Will for me
Yet Lord I know my heart
Come Lord reveal to me today
Show me my life....my part

I want to be so right Dear Lord
I want to walk with You
Lord I'm hurting and confused though now
My faith is failing too

I know You have a plan...yes Lord
I know it works out right
Give me some peace of mind Oh Lord
To help me through this night

Proverbs 16:3

Commit to the LORD whatever you do,
and he will establish your plans.

Wrong Lead

Lord please, I tell You of a question
Reveal the answer now to me
How does man minister to Your People
When that man's work no one can see

How do you minister to the married
When you are struggling on number three
How do you teach a person fitness
When you are out of shape to be

How do you minister to the weak
When you are struggling to be strong
How do you teach about the Spirit
When every scripture you quote is wrong

How do you continue to use the church
As your holy pedestal...promoting self
How do you say it's for God's people
Then you just take till nothing's left

Lord I don't understand this mindset
How in this can Christ be manifest
Lord let me know what lead to follow
So I know how to give my best

I will look to You Lord, always
I will let the filter be Your Word
And as I gain more of Your Wisdom
I'll make sure it's **Your Voice** that is heard

Your Time

Oh Jesus how I come to You
As others when I'm down
Oh Jesus how I ask for help
As the emotions of life go around

But Jesus now I come to You
With no thoughts of only self
And Jesus I am standing firm
As Your servant with no one left

I come to You with hands apart
Not asking You to give
But thanking You for all the love
And for allowing me to live

I raise my arms in celebrant
My praise goes out to Thee
And even though I still need help
This time is not about me

I don't want to ask for anything
I just want to spread Your Fame
I just want to praise and worship You
I just want to lift Your Name

So I thank You now
For all You've done
I thank You now for me
And I'll lift and praise and worship You
So that all the world will see

Psalm 34:1

I will bless the LORD at all times: his praise shall continually be in my mouth.

Walking with Divine Intervention

Inspiring phrases to enlighten your walk with God; fresh thoughts to help lift your burdens and challenge you to get closer to the Word. And by doing so, get closer to our Lord and Savior, Jesus Christ!

B. Chuck Thomas
"TheOldPoetHimself"

www.ingramcontent.com/pod-product-compliance
Lightning Source LLC
Chambersburg PA
CBHW070913030726
47504CB00005B/1575